The Egyptian Conception of Immortality

George Andrew Reisner

Contents

THE EGYPTIAN
CONCEPTION
OF IMMORTALITY

BY

George Andrew Reisner

THE INGERSOLL LECTURESHIP

Extract from the will of Miss Caroline Haskell Ingersoll, who died in Keene, County of Cheshire, New Hampshire, Jan. 26, 1893.

First.   In carrying out the wishes of my late beloved father, George Goldthwait Ingersoll, as declared by him in his last will and testament, I give and bequeath to Harvard University in Cambridge, Mass., where my late father was graduated, and which he always held in love and honor, the sum of Five thousand dollars ($5,000) as a fund for the establishment of a Lectureship on a plan somewhat similar to that of the Dudleian lecture, that is--one lecture to be delivered each year, on any convenient day between the last of May and the first day of December, on this subject, "the Immortality of Man," said lecture not to form a part of the usual college course, nor to be delivered by any Professor or Tutor as part of his usual routine of instruction, though any such Professor or Tutor may be appointed to such service. The choice of said lecturer is not to be limited to any one religious denomination, nor to any one profession, but may be that of either clergyman or layman, the appointment to take place at least six months before the delivery of said lecture. The above sum to be safely invested and three fourths of the annual interest thereof to be paid to the lecturer for his services and the remaining fourth to be expended in the publishment and gratuitous distribution of the lecture, a copy of which is always to be furnished by the lecturer for such purpose. The same lecture to be named and known as the "the Ingersoll lecture on the Immortality of Man."

I. INTRODUCTION

Of the nations which have contributed to the direct stream of civilization, Egypt and Mesopotamia are at present believed to be the oldest. The chronological dispute as to the relative antiquity of the two countries is of minor importance; for while in Babylonia the historical material is almost entirely inscriptional, in Egypt we know the handicrafts, the weapons, the arts, and, to a certain extent, the religious beliefs of the race up to a period when it was just emerging from the Stone Age. In a word, Egypt presents the most ancient race whose manner of life is known to man. From the beginning of its history--that is, from about 4500 B.C.--we can trace the development of a religion one of whose most prominent elements was a promise of a life after death. It was still a great religion when the Christian doctrine of immortality was enunciated. In the early centuries of the Christian era, it seemed almost possible that the worship of Osiris and Isis might become the religion of the classical world; and the last stand made by civilized paganism against Christianity was in the temple of Isis at Philae in the sixth century after Christ.

It is clear that a religion of such duration must have offered some of those consolations to man that have marked all great religions, chief of which is the faith in a spirit, in something that preserves the personality of the man and does not perish with the body. This faith was, in fact, one of the chief elements in the Egyptian religion--the element best known to us through the endless cemeteries which fill the desert from one end of Egypt to the other, and through the funerary inscriptions.

It is necessary, however, to correct the prevailing impression that religion played the greatest part in Egyptian life or even a greater part than it does in Moslem Egypt. The mistaken belief that death and the well-being of the dead overshadowed the existence of the living, is due to the fact that the physical character of the country has preserved for us the cemeteries and the funerary temples better than all the other monuments. The narrow strip of fat black land along the Nile produces generally its three crops a year. It is much too valuable to use as a cemetery. But more than that, it is subject to periodic saturation with water during the inundation, and is, therefore, unsuitable for the burials of a nation which wished to preserve the contents of the graves. On the other hand, the desert, which bounds this fertile strip so closely that a dozen steps will usually carry one from the black land to the gray,--the desert offers a dry preserving soil with absolutely no value to the living. Thus all the funerary monuments were erected on the desert, and except where intentionally destroyed they are preserved to the present day. The palaces, the towns, the farms, and many of the great temples which were erected on the black soil, have been pulled down for building material or buried deep under the steadily rising deposits of the Nile. The tombs of six thousand years of dead have accumulated on the desert edge.

Moreover, our impression of these tombs has been formed from the monuments erected by kings, princes, priests, and the great and wealthy men of the kingdom. The multitude of plain unadorned burial-places which the scientific excavator records by the thousands have escaped the attention of scholars interested in Egypt from the point of view of a comparison of religions. It has also been overlooked that the strikingly colored mummies and the glaring burial apparatus of the late period cost very little to prepare. The manufacture of mummies was a regular trade in the Ptolemaic period at least. Mummy cases were prepared in advance with blank spaces for the names. I do not think that any more expense was incurred in Egyptian funerals in the dynastic period than is the case among the modern Egyptians. The importance of the funerary rites to the living must, therefore, not be exaggerated.

II. SOURCES OF THE MATERIAL

With the exception of certain mythological explanations supplied by the inscriptions and reliefs in the temples, our knowledge of Egyptian ideas in regard to the future life is based on funerary customs as revealed by excavations and on the funerary texts found in the tombs. These tombs always show the same essential functions through all changes of form,--the protection of the burial against decay and spoliation, and the provision of a meeting-place where the living may bring offerings to the dead. Correspondingly, there are two sets of customs,--burial customs and offering customs. The texts follow the same division. For the offering place, the texts are magical formulas which, properly recited by the living, provide material benefit for the dead. For the burial place, the texts are magical formulas to be used by the spirit for its own benefit in the difficulties of the spirit life. These texts from the burial chambers are found in only a few graves,--those of the very great,--and their contents show us that they were intended only for people whose earthly position was exceptional.

From the funerary customs and the offering texts, a clear view is obtained of the general conception, the ordinary practice. We see what was regarded as absolutely essential to the belief of the common man. From the texts found in the burial chambers we get the point of view of the educated or powerful man, the things that might be done to gain for him an exceptional place in the other world. Both of these classes of material must be considered, in order to gain a true idea of the practical beliefs. For it must be emphasized from the beginning that we have in Egypt several apparently conflicting conceptions of immortality. Nor are we anywhere near obtaining in the case of the texts the clearness necessary to understand fully all the differing views held by the priestly classes during a period of over two thousand years.

III. THE IDEAS OF THE PRIMITIVE RACE

The earliest belief in immortality is that which is shown to us by the burial customs of the primitive race,--the prehistoric Egyptian race.

About 4500 B.C. we find the Egyptian race was just emerging from the Stone Age. All the implements and weapons found are of flint or other stone. The men of that time were ignorant of writing, but show a certain facility in line drawings of men, plants, and animals. We have found thousands of their graves which all show the same idea of death. Each person was buried with implements, weapons, ornaments,--no doubt those actually used in life,-- with a full outfit of household pots and pans, and with a supply of food. The man was dead, but he still needed the same things he used in ordinary life. By a fortunate chance we have even recovered bodies accidentally desiccated and preserved intact in the dry soil. These bodies do not show any trace of mutilation, mummification, or any other preparation for the grave except probably washing. The dead body was simply laid on a mat in the grave, covered with a cloth and a mat or a skin, and then with clean gravel. But with it was placed all those things which the man might need if his life were to go on in some mysterious, unseen way, as life went on among those on earth. Possibly his relations as in later times brought offerings of food to the grave, but here even the dry soil of Egypt fails to furnish positive evidence. All this shows a plain simple belief in the persistence of the life of a man as distinguished from the body --a belief widely prevalent among primitive people. It contains nothing unusual, and is probably perfectly explicable psychologically by means of dreams.

There is little or no change in this underlying belief to be observed in the burial customs of the Egyptians during the late predynastic period. Copper weapons and implements succeed stone in the graves. All those objects in whose manufacture the new tools are used show changes of technique and form. It is even curious to note that some of the older stone and flint objects, some of the older pots and pans, are still made as a matter of tradition. The importance of this is not to be overlooked. For centuries men had used flint knives and they had baked their bread in flat mud saucers set in the ashes. For the centuries these flint knives and these cakes with their saucers had been placed in the graves. Gradually metal knives and better bread pans displaced these more primitive objects in daily life; but the older primitive objects were still placed in the graves as a matter of tradition.

It must be remembered, of course, that these traditional objects were also in use in ancient traditional ceremonies on earth. The sacrificial animals were still slaughtered with flint knives. The old-style cakes were still offered in the holy places. In other words, life on earth now consisted of ordinary material life and a traditional life--a life that clung to the forms of a more primitive civilization as somehow more effective with the divine powers. This view is closely reflected in the grave furniture; here, too, were the practical objects and the traditional ceremonial objects. Life after death is still always the same as life on earth--with the same physical needs, with the same need of help from supernatural powers or against supernatural powers. The spirit of the man needed the spirit of the copper axe to swing in battle; but just as much he needed the spirit of the flint knife to make the first cut across the throat of the spirit bull of sacrifice. Remember this--the other world, in which lived the spirit of the dead, was filled with the spirits or ghosts of all things and animals. The other, the unseen, was a duplicate of this world; all things which have shape were there --even to the black fields and the broad river of Egypt. This is the foundation of the Egyptian conception of immortality. Through all the modifications and accretions of the following three thousand years, this foundation idea is always clearly visible. All the statues, the carved and painted tombs, all the curious little model boats and workshops, all the painted mummies, all the amulets, the scarabs, the little funerary statuettes,--all this mummery which seems to be so characteristic and so essential, is only the means to an end, and an ever changing means to secure a successful comfortable existence of the spirit in the life after death,--in the ghostly duplicate of life on earth.

IV. THE EARLY DYNASTIC PERIOD

It is clear that the effort to attain an immortality which is merely a ghostly continuation of life on earth must reflect the general development of Egyptian culture,--especially the advance in arts and crafts. One of the most striking examples of this fact is the introduction of metal working mentioned above and the consequent placing of both flint and copper in the grave, --the division of grave furniture into practical objects and ceremonial objects, which is the foundation for the use of symbolic objects in later times.

The advance in arts and crafts not only suggests new ideas of the necessities of the spirit, but it provides the necessary technical skill for the more effective satisfaction of all the needs of the dead. This takes, first of all, the form of supplying a place for the burial, which furnishes greater security to the body and a better communication between the living and the dead.

From the First Dynasty, say from 3300 B.C. down, as soon as the Egyptian had mastered the use of mud-brick and wood, we gain the certainty of an idea which could only be guessed at in the primitive period. A place is provided above the grave at which the living could meet the spirit of the dead with *periodical* offerings of food and other necessities. In the life after death, spirit food and drink, once used, ceased to be, just as in life on earth, and had to be renewed from day to day, lest the spirit of the dead suffer from hunger and thirst. One of the great developments of the first six dynasties looked to the provision of these daily necessities.

The invention of writing was immediately utilized. About the beginning of the First Dynasty writing was invented for administrative and other practical purposes. Gravestones, bearing in relief the name of the dead, were set up in the offering places of the kings and court people. These were probably reminders for use in some simple formula recited in presenting the periodical offerings. As the Egyptians became more familiar with the use of writing, the offering formula was written out in full, enlarged and modified.

Sculptures, both relief and statuary, in every stage of their development, were used as magical accessories to the offering rites.

So, also, the whole history of Egyptian architecture was reflected in the tomb; for every advance brought about some change in the form or structure. In fact, the whole development of the form of the Egyptian tomb depended on the development of technical skill. The same funerary functions are served throughout. As all the great artisans were at the command of the king, all the great technical discoveries and inventions were first made in his service. But every permanent gain in knowledge was a benefit to the race and utilized by the common people. So, for example, the skill acquired in stone-cutting, during the construction of the great pyramids, was utilized a little later in producing rock-cut tombs from one end of Egypt to the other.

The functions of the grave remained the same. Yet with the changes in form resulting from the growth of skill, modifications in the funerary customs crept in.

The mud-brick tombs of the early part of the First Dynasty, like the pre-dynastic graves, had only one chamber, limited in size by the length of logs obtainable to form the roof. The growing desire for ostentation found a way to enlarge the tombs by building them with a number of chambers. The burial was placed in the central chamber and the burial furniture in the additional chambers. In this way the separation of the furniture and the actual burial was brought about.

V. THE OLD EMPIRE

Another change comes in the Fourth Dynasty, and is to be noted first in the royal tombs, as is always the case. The Egyptians had now learned to cut stone and build with it. The burial chambers hollowed in the solid rock were necessarily smaller than the old chambers dug in the gravel and no longer sufficient to contain the great mass of furniture gathered by a king for his grave. On the other hand, the chapels with the increase in architectural skill could be build of great size. Corresponding to these technical conditions we find a great increase in the importance of the chapel. It becomes a great temple, whose magazines were filled with all those objects which had formerly been placed in the burial chamber and were so necessary to the life of the spirit. The temples of the third pyramid, for example, contained nearly two thousand stone vessels. Great estates were set aside by will, and the income appointed to the support of certain persons who on their side were obliged to keep up the temple, to make the offerings and to recite the magical formulas which would provide the spirit with all its necessities.

Following closely the growth in importance of the royal chapels, the private offering places assumed a greater importance. The custom of periodic offerings and the use of magical texts grew until it reached its highest point in the Fifth Dynasty. At this time there is a burial chamber deep underground where the dead was laid securely in ancient traditional attitude, with his clothing and a few personal ornaments. As a rule, it is only the women, always conservative, that have anything more. Above this grave, there is a solid rectangular structure, with a chapel or offering place on the side towards the valley. The offering place is always there, no matter how poor or small the tomb. But to understand just what the Egyptian thought, we must turn to the better tombs. The walls are of limestone carved with reliefs representing the important processes of daily life,--sowing, reaping, cattle-herding, hunting, pot-making, weaving,--all those actions which furnish the daily supplies. The dead man is represented overseeing all this. Finally, near the offering niche, he is represented seated, usually with his wife at a table bearing loaves of the traditional *ta* bread. Beside him are represented heaps of provisions--meat, cakes, vegetables, wine and beer. A list of objects is never missing, marked with numbers,--a thousand loaves of bread, a thousand head of cattle, a thousand jars of wine, a thousand garments, and so on. We know from latter inscriptions that these words, properly recited, created for the spirit a store of spirit objects in equal numbers. Below the niche is an altar for receiving actual offerings of food and drink. It is clear that the living, coming to this offering place with or without material offerings, could, by proper recitation, secure to the spirit of the dead all its daily needs. This offering niche is the door of the other world --symbolically and actually. In many graves the niche is carved to represent a door--sometimes opening in, and sometimes opening out. Moreover, in several cases the figure of the dead is carved half emerging from the opening door--a figure in all ways like the figure of the dead as he is represented in the scenes from life. Beyond this door lives the spirit of the dead.

In many offering chambers there is a small hole in the wall, either in the offering niche or in another place. If this hole be properly lighted and the space beyond has not been changed by decay or violation, the light falls on the face of a statue of the dead looking forth to the world of the living. For behind the wall is another chamber, closed except for this small hole. This hidden chamber contains statues of the dead often accompanied by statues of his family and his servants. These statues of the dead are labeled with his name, and are said to be the abode of his spirit, his *ka*, as the Egyptians called it. Moreover, all the offering formulas named the *ka* as the recipient of the food and drink. The duplicate spirit of the man is his *ka*. In these statues we have, then, a simulacrum of the man provided for use of his *ka*--perhaps to assist the *ka* to the persistence of his earthly form, and to the remembrance of his name. But what were the uses of the subsidiary statues? What spirit resided in them? The man's son in his turn died, and a similar room was made for him with his statue and his subsidiary statues. Did his *ka* live both in the statue placed with his father's statue and also in the statue in his own grave? We have no answer. Probably the Egyptian mind never formulated the difficulty.

But the new idea is clearly expressed. It is no longer necessary to fill the burial chamber with a mass of household furniture for the use of the dead. All these things can be carved on the wall of the burial chamber and so made effective for his use. It was in any case necessary to supply his food by means of the offerings, and it was quite as easy to supply all his other necessities in the same way. In other words, there is a distinct growth in the use of magic to benefit the dead. At the same time, we find the growth of the custom of supplying a special abode for the *ka*--a simulacrum of the man, which assisted the *ka* to retain the form of the living man and to remember his identity.

The tendency of this period is then to place a greater dependence on magic than on food, drink, and grave furniture. It is, therefore, not surprising to find introduced, for the first time, the use of magical texts in the burial chamber,--the so-called Pyramid Texts. In the burial chamber in the pyramid of Unas, last king of the Fifth Dynasty, and in the pyramids of the kings of the Sixth Dynasty, the walls are covered with long magical texts or chapters--the oldest form of the so-called book of the dead or "book of the going forth by day." The texts were probably somewhat older, but are now used for the first time in this manner, no doubt owing to the increased facility in carving stone. In these the various powers of the other world are invoked by the incidents of the Osiris-Isis legend, to preserve the dead body, to feed the *ka*, and to assist the other spirit, the *ba*, in its struggles with supernatural powers.

The pyramid texts introduce us to three important ideas,--(1) a curious plurality of the spirit existence, (2) a condition of immortality better than that of the old underworld or Earu, and (3) most important of all, the identification of the king with Osiris according to the terms of the Osiris-Isis legend.

In all the older offering formulas it is only the *ka* spirit which is mentioned. Here is the body perishable and destructible; here is the life, the *ka* which fills every limb and vessel of the body and must, therefore, have the same form. When death comes, the *ka* spirit, the image of the man, remains near the body, and this spirit it was which was the object of the rites and offerings in the funerary chapel. But besides this *ka*, it appears for the first time that the king at any rate possesses also a soul called a *ba*. In later times we see that every man possessed a *ba*, and we learn that each god possessed several *ba's*. But it is in the pyramid texts that we learn for the first time of the *ba* of a man, and that man is a king. When death comes, the *ba* takes flight in the form of a bird or whatever form it wills. All seems confused.

The *ka* was near the body, the *ka* was in the field of Earu, under the earth ploughing and sowing; the *ba* is fluttering on the branches of the tree on earth, the *ba* has fled like a falcon to the heavens, and has been set as a star among the stars. The dead king lives with the gods and is fed by them. The goddesses give him the breast. He lives in the Island of Food. He lives in Earu, the Underworld, a land like Egypt, with fields and canals and flood and harvest. He shares with the gods in the offerings made in the great temples on earth.

It is quite clear that all this is an expression of dissatisfaction with the old belief in the simple duplicate world, the world of Earu under the earth. It is noteworthy that this first appears in royal tombs. These texts are written for kings alone. It is only many centuries later that the texts of the book of the dead showed similar possibilities open to the common man. This is the usual course of all advances in Egypt,-- architecture, sculpture, writing, whatever gain in skill or knowledge there is, appears first in the service of the royal family. Thus, even in the conception of immortality, the new ideas, the better immortality was first thought out for the benefit of the king. The basis for this lay simply in the life on earth. The king had come early to have a sort of divinity ascribed to him. His chief name was the Horus name. Menes was the Horus Aha; Cheops was the Horus Mejeru; Pepy II was the Horus Netery-khau. But he was also the son of Ra, the sun-god, endued with life forever. The king was a god, and it could only be that in his future life he shared the life of the gods. Thus, all is no more confused or mysterious than is the conception of the life of the gods themselves.

But the texts go even further than this and identify the dead god-man, who as Horus was king on earth, with the father of Horus, the dead god of the earth, Osiris. This identification of the dead man with the dead god Osiris was later enlarged to include all men, and became in the Ptolemaic period the most characteristic feature of the Egyptian conception of life after death.

The Osiris story as it can be pieced together from the pyramid texts [See A. Erman: *Die Aegyptische Religion*, p. 38 ff.] was briefly thus: Keb, the earth-god, and Nut, the goddess of the sky, had four children,-- Osiris and Isis, Seth and Nephthys,-- who were thus paired in marriage. Keb gave Osiris his dominion, the earth, and made him the god of the earth, and he ruled justly and powerfully. Seth, his brother, was jealous, and by treachery enticed Osiris into a box, which he closed and threw into the water. Isis sought for the body of her husband until she found it, and Isis and Nephthys, her sister, sat at his head and feet and bewailed him. Re, the greatest of the gods, heard Isis's complaint; his heart was touched, and he sent Anubis to bury Osiris. Anubis rejoined his separated bones, bound him with cloths, and prepared him for burial,--that is, mummified him. This is the form in which Osiris is represented,--as a mummy. Isis then fanned her wings, and the air from her wings caused the mummy to live. His life on earth, however, was over, could not be recalled, so that his new life could only be passed in the other world, the world of the dead. Here Osiris became king, as he had been king on earth. But Isis conceived from the dead-living Osiris, bore a child in secret, and suckled him, hidden in a swamp. When the child, the sun-god Horus, grew up, he fought against Seth to recover his father's kingdom, and to avenge his death. Both gods were injured in the fight. Horus lost an eye. But Thoth intervened, separated the fighters, and healed their wounds. Thoth spat upon the eye of Horus and it became whole. Horus, however, gave his eye to Osiris to eat, and thereby Osiris became endowed with life, soul, and power (i.e. in the underworld). But Seth disputed the legitimacy of the birth of Horus, and the great gods held a court in the house of Keb. In this court, justice was done, the truth of Horus's claims was established, and he was placed on the throne of his father. Osiris became the ruler in the land of the dead, Horus in the land of the living.

The kernel of the story appears to be this: Osiris is the god of the earth, and his life is the life of the vegetation, dying and reviving with the course of the seasons, mourned by his wife Isis and succeeded by his son Horus, the sun-god. It is apparently a form of the common Tammuz or Adonis story of the Semites. This fact brings with it a suggestion which requires consideration.

The racial connection of the Egyptians may seem to have little to do with immortality. But I beg a moment's consideration. The two great dominating ideas of immortality are those held by the Christians and by the Mohammedans, and these are essentially the same idea. Both these religions are creations of the Semitic race. It is, therefore, decidedly of importance to find that the Egyptian race, the creator of a third great religion, has also a large Semitic strain. In fact, the investigations of the last ten years appear to show that this Semitic strain it was which gave the Egyptian race its creative power and made possible the development of the Egyptian civilization.

The Egyptian language furnishes us with indisputable proof of the Semitic affinity, as Professor Adolf Erman showed years ago. The anatomical examination by Professor Elliot Smith of a large number of skeletons, dated by careful excavations, has given us a further clue. There is a prehistoric race found in the earliest cemeteries--neither Negroid nor Asiatic in characteristics. In the late predynastic and the early dynastic periods, when the great development began, this primitive race had become modified by an infiltration of broad-headed people from the north. In the Old Empire, this broad-headed people had become predominant, and remain so throughout all Lower and Middle Egypt until the present day. This intruding race, whose advent marks the beginning of Egyptian civilization, I believe to have been Semitic.

Remember this--the texts show clearly older ideas in conflict with the Osiris belief. The primitive race was not, I believe, a race of Osiris followers. Professor Erman has stated that the Osiris belief is as early as 4200 B.C. That I am certain is absolutely untenable. It is a question of Egyptian chronology in which I beg to differ radically both from Eduard Meyer and Professor Erman. In the formal calendar year of three hundred and sixty-five days, there are twelve months of thirty days and five intercalary days. These intercalary days are called the birthdays of Osiris, Horus, Seth, Isis, and Nephthys--the five most important figures in the Osiris myth. According to Professor Meyer and Professor Erman, this formal calendar was introduced in 4200 B.C., one of the occasions when the heliacal rising of the star Sothis fell on the first of the month Thoth of the calendar. However, if we accept with them the date 3300 B.C. as the date of the First dynasty, then in 4200 B.C. the Egyptians were just emerging from a neolithic state. They were culturally incapable of making a formal calendar and could have no possible use for one. Either the calendar did not originate in Egypt, or it was introduced in 2780 B.C., when again the heliacal rising Sothis fell on the first of Thoth. At this time the Osiris story was dominant, in the religion. We have a race almost certainly Semitic, fusing the primitive race during the period 3500-3000, and a few centuries later we have a new religious idea dominating the fused race. When we examine this new idea, the Osiris belief, we find its earliest form nothing more nor less than the common tammuz or Adonis story of the Semites. The conclusion lies very near at hand, that the Osiris story is in fact the Tammuz story, brought into Egypt by the earliest Semitic tribes. In any case it was a race with a large Semitic mixture which utilized this story in working out a theory of immortality; and in all probability we have in the Osiris-Isis religion a third great religion due to the Semitic race.

However this may be, it is clear that the craving of the king for a special immortality, for an exalted future life, found its justification through the Osiris-Isis myth. Horus was the successor of Osiris as lord of the earth and the living. The kings of Egypt were the successors of Horus. The chief name of the king was his Horus name; Menes was the Horus Aha, Cheops the Horus Mejeru. When the king died, he became Osiris, and passed to the kingdom of Osiris. He passed through the underworld with the sun-god, abode there as Osiris, the god-king, or sped to the heavens to the celestial gods. Thus comes the entering wedge of a great change in the conception of immortality--an ordinary immortality for the common man, a special divine immortality for the divine man, the king. [It appears probable that the deification of the king and the assumption of a divine immortality for him was prior in time to the statement of these beliefs in the terms of the Osiris story.] Even at this early age, it was, of course, clearly stated that the king must be righteous, morally satisfactory in the eyes of the world and of the gods. The gods, as always, were on the side of the moral code, and especially on the side of the organized religion. It is perhaps significant that the chief sins of the kings of the Fourth dynasty, so execrated by the Egyptian priests in the Ptolemaic period, were sins against the great gods. The other charges are for the most part plainly slanders. In practice every king whose family remained in power was justified before gods and men, and took his place among the gods in the islands of the blessed in the northern part of the heavens.

The dead body was laid in the grave, supplied with all these magic texts which were to restore and revive the soul and guide it across waters and through dangers to the place of Osiris. But the chapel was not wanting, the cult of the *ka* was maintained, the statues were placed in the hidden room, the food and drink were brought daily to the door of the grave. Thus, while a special immortality was evolved for the king, the funeral customs continue to show the same service of the *ka* as in the earlier period.

In the Sixth Dynasty, there is a return to the older practice of placing objects in the grave itself. At present we are unable to point out the reasons for this. Possibly experience had taught men that endowments and craved walls left to the care of descendants were insecure supports for a life after death which was to last forever. At any rate, the custom arose of making small models in wood or stone or metal of those scenes and objects which were carved in relief on the walls of the chapel, --models of houses, granaries, of kitchens, of brickyards; models of herds and servants and soldiers; models of boats and ships; models of dance-halls with the man seated drinking wine, around him musicians, before him dancing girls; models of swords, of vessels, of implements. Poorer people must be contented with poorer things, down to the peasant who is buried with the few little necessary pots and pans of his daily life. But always, in every grave, the chapel, small or great, is there. The endowment of funerary priests continues. Every man, I suppose, however poor, had some one to make at least one offering at his grave. And so it was down to the New Empire.

VI. THE MIDDLE EMPIRE

During the Middle Empire, the burial and offering customs show the persistence of the old belief in life after death as on earth. Pots, vessels, tools, weapons, ornaments, clothing, and models of scenes from life, continue to be placed in the burial chamber. The walls of the offering chambers of the nobles, at this time cut in the rock, still bear representations from life carved in relief. The symbolical doors and the offering formulas still mark the spot where the dead receive the necessities of life from the living. All graves of every class testify to the faith in a life after death similar to life on earth. Yet certain modifications are apparent which are significant for the future development of the conception of immortality: (1) the pyramid texts are used by the provincial nobles for their own benefit; (2) Abydos assumes a great importance as the burial place of Osiris; (3) the swathed mummy comes into general use in burials.

The first identification of the king with Osiris in the pyramid texts marks the conception of a better immortality for him. So, as the possibility of a better immortality was claimed by wider and wider circles of men, the use of the pyramid texts, or similar texts, also became wider. In the Middle Empire, texts practically identical with the pyramid texts, but furnished with illustrations somewhat like those of the later books of the dead, are found in the coffins of provincial nobles.

The power of the monarchy had been weakening during the Fifth and Sixth Dynasties, partly owing to the dissipation of national resources by royal extravagance, partly owing to other causes. After the Sixth Dynasty, the country was clearly in a period of economic depression; and the government was broken up into a series of nearly independent baronies corresponding roughly to the later division into provinces or nomes. Our material is scanty. The tombs of very few great men have been found. But when in the Twelfth Dynasty an abundance of material is at hand, we see, alongside the old forms of the burial customs, the use of the pyramid texts on the inside walls of the coffins of the great man. It was now possible for the *ba* of the great landed noble to seek refuge with the gods in the northwest heavens and share their life.

The increasing importance of Abydos as the burial place of Osiris is of still greater significance. The tomb of a king of the First Dynasty was identified by the priests as the actual burial place of Osiris. Many great people made graves for themselves in the same field; or, if they lived at a distance, built empty cenotaphs there. A great temple of Osiris stood near by, and became the centre of the celebration of mysteries illustrating the death and revival of Osiris. Fortunately, a certain high official named I-kher-nofret has left us an account of the Osiris passion-play as performed under his oversight in the nineteenth year of Sesostris III, nearly two thousand years before Christ [See Schafer's article, "Die Osiris-mysterien," in Sethe's ***Untersuchungen zur Geshichte Aegyptens***, IV, 2, pp 1-42.]. The play began by the procession of the statue of the jackal-god Wep-wawet (the road-opener) going forth to help his father Osiris. Then the statue of Osiris himself in the Neshemet boat came forth as triumphant king of the earth. Sham battles took place referring to the conquest of the earth by Osiris. These processions were only introductory. The principal procession took place on the following day (or days), when Osiris went forth to his death at Nedit. The actual death scene certainly took place in secret. But when the dead body was found, the multitude joined in the wailing and the lamentations. The god Thoth went forth in a boat and brought back the body of Osiris. The body was prepared for burial and taken in funeral procession to the grave at Peker. Osiris was avenged on his enemies in a great battle on the water at Nedit. Finally, the god, his life revived, comes from Peker in triumphant procession and enters his temple at Abydos.

Osiris mysteries were celebrated at other places, at least in later times and perhaps even in the Middle Empire; but it is not easy to discern the part these mysteries played in the Middle Empire in the beliefs of the common people regarding their immortality. The Osiris story was one of the most widespread in Egypt, and, powerful in its effect on the feelings of all classes, was certain, sooner or later, to prepare the way for a general belief in a better immortality; but if we may judge from the burial customs, the great mass of the people still believed merely in an underworld, Earu, a duplicate of the earthly life, but with greater possibilities of danger and evil.

During the course of Egyptian history the position in which the body is buried undergoes a series of remarkable changes. During the early pre-dynastic period, the body, loosely enfolded in cloths and skins, is laid in the grave double up on the left side, *usually* with the head south (i.e. upstream). This position becomes the custom, with very few exceptions, during the late predynastic period and the first three dynasties. Throughout the Fourth to Sixth Dynasties, the body was in the same position, but with the head north, loosely covered with shawls and garments. The crouching position, with some slight modifications, continues to be used for the poorest class down to the New Empire. Among the Nubians, it is universal to the New Empire and customary even later in unmixed Nubian communities. The swathed extended burials begin in Egypt in the Fourth Dynasty, so far as remains are preserved. Some members of the royal family of Cheops were buried in swathed wrapping, lying extended on the left side with the knees bent. During the Fifth and Sixth Dynasties this extended position on the side becomes customary for the better classes; and during the Middle Empire it becomes almost universal.

The final burial position, the swathed mummy lying extended on the back, does not become general until the New Empire, about 1600 B.C. although it is the position hitherto regarded as the characteristic Egyptian burial position. A few isolated cases, some of them perhaps accidental, occur as early as the Old Empire; but in the New Empire the extended burial on the back is practically the only one to be observed. In other words, beginning in the predynastic period with a burial position which may be called natural and primitive, the Egyptian gradually adopted a position which imitated the form of the dead Osiris, the god of the dead. Each new change is first adopted by the royal family, and is taken up by the other classes in turn until it becomes universal. In the final form, the mummy was a simulacrum of the dead as Osiris.

Alongside these changes in the burial position progressed the art of preserving the body. The earliest attempts were made on the body of the king; and the knowledge of embalming gained in preserving his body was gradually utilized for the higher classes and finally for all but the poorest. It seems indisputable that the royal personages of the Fourth and Sixth Dynasties were mummified--i.e., the entrails were drawn, the body prepared with spices and resins and wrapped tightly in cloths smeared with resin. But the mummies of the nobles, even of this period, show no trace of such treatment. The receptacles for the viscera are sometimes found in their graves in the Sixth Dynasty, but are, as a rule, empty, being mere dummy vases. Even in the Middle Empire, the preservation of the bodies of the better classes was extremely imperfect. The bundles of wrappings have kept their form to the present day and it seems as if the mummy were still intact; but an examination of the interior shows only loose bones. Successful mummification appears among better-class people in the New Empire for the first time and becomes a general custom in the Late Period. The processes of successful mummification necessitated the practical destruction of the body.

In the Middle Empire, which is the period under discussion, the process of mummification had reached a middle stage, and, while we are unable to explain exactly the causal relationship, it is clear that this advance in the treatment of the body accompanied a spread of the belief in the Osirian immortality.

VII. THE NEW EMPIRE

The New Empire (1600-1200 B.C.) was the great period of foreign conquest. The Hyksos, Asiatic invaders, had held Egypt for a century or more. The Theban princes who drove them out became kings of Egypt, and followed them into Asia. With an army trained in war by the long struggle with the Hyksos, the Egyptian kings, having tasted the sweetness of the spoils of war, entered on the conquest of western Asia and the Sudan. The plunder of both these regions poured into Egypt. Under Thothmes III an annual campaign was conducted into Syria to bring back the spoils and the tribute. Foreign slaves and the products of foreign handicraft were for sale in every market-place. The treasury was filled to overflowing. A large share was assigned to Amon, the god of the Theban family. Temples were built for him; estates established for the maintenance of his rites; thousands of priests enrolled for the service of his properties. The god became, in a material sense, the greatest god of Egypt, the national god; and his priesthood became the most powerful organization in the kingdom. The high priest of Amon usurped the power of the king and finally supplanted him. Such was the period in which the next great development of the Egyptian idea of immortality is to be noted-- a period of priestly activity in the beginning and of priestly domination in the end.

The priests are the scribes, the men of learning. They have the lore of all magic, medicine, rules of conduct, religious rites. It is not mere chance, therefore, that the New Empire was marked by a great increase of magic in all its forms--texts and symbolic objects--and by a great development in the knowledge of the other world. In some of the texts the geography of the underworld, in which Osiris is king, is worked out in great detail. When the sun sets in the west, Ra in his boat enters the underworld and passes through it during the twelve hours of the night, bringing light and happiness to those who are in the underworld. In the effort to secure the tomb against plundering, the royal graves had been cut in the solid rock,--long and complicated passages with false leads and deceptive turns and the burial chamber in an unexpected place. The long walls of these rooms presented a great surface suitable to decoration, and they were utilized to depict scenes from the underworld and the passage of Ra through it, so that the tombs became in fact representations of the land of the dead, and were so considered. These royal tombs were at a distance from the cultivated land, hidden in valleys in the desert. Their funerary temples were built on the edge of the desert beside the temples of the gods of the place.

Such fantastical reconstructions of the other world, however, never found general favor and are confined to a few royal tombs. The priests and other prominent people have rolls of papyrus buried with them, bearing copies of books of the dead. These books of the dead are made up of a series of chapters, each complete in itself and each dealing with some phase of the future life. There is no set order of chapters. There is no fixed number of chapters. Each scribe seems to have selected the chapters which he considered useful. The general title is: Chapters of the going forth by day. The general character may be given by a paragraph attached to one of the chapters in the Book of Ani the Scribe [Edited by E. A. W. Budge, p. 26]: "If this book be known on earth and written on the coffin, it is my mouth. He shall come forth by day in any form he desires and he shall go into his place without being prevented. There shall be given to him bread and beer and meat upon the altar of Osiris. He shall enter in, in peace, to the field of Earu according to this decree of the one who is in the City of Dedu. There shall be given to him wheat and barley there. He shall flourish as he did upon earth. He shall do his desires like these nine Gods who are in the underworld, as found true millions of times. He is the Osiris: the Scribe Ani."

There are chapters to overcome all the evil which a soul may encounter; there are words to greet all the gods whom the soul desires to visit. The Scribe Ani had an exceptional position on earth; he desires to do his desire in the other world; and in the names of Osiris he recites the magic words that bring him the power. He is Ani, but he calls himself Osiris; just as the priestly doctor mixes his dose of medicine and calls it "the eye of Horus tested and found true."

In addition to magical texts, there are also magical, or symbolic, objects placed in the graves,--amulets of various kinds which were to be used in the other world. Some of these were simply the amulets used in daily life to guard against sickness, bite of snake, and other earthly evils which were also incident to the life after death. Other amulets, like the so-called *Ushabtiu*, were to meet special conditions of the other world. These *Ushabtiu*, or "answerers," were little images of workmen bearing agricultural implements whose duty it was to take the place of the dead in the fields of Earu when Osiris as king called him to do his share of the field work. Even the king appears liable to this service, and for him thousands of these figures were made,--sometimes labeled each with the day of the year. In a few cases there was even a charm written on the figure to prevent it hearing the command of any one but its master.

Alongside these manifold manifestations of the belief in magic, other furniture--implements, weapons, and utensils--are still placed in the grave. The offering places are still maintained. All burials are now extended on the back and wrapped in bandages. Yet the common graves lack the receptacles for the viscera, lack magical texts, lack ushabtiu, and--in a word--lack all those things which are typical of the better-class graves of the period. The conception of the future life among the common people is apparently not essentially different from that of the Old Empire. But the books of the dead and the offering formulas show that the priests and high officials at death were called Osiris.

By the end of the Late Period the Osiris cult of the dead had come to be universal. No doubt political events had much to do with this. The absorption of the powers of the king by the priesthood of the national god Amon-Ra, the crushing of the nobility by a succession of foreign invaders, and the general uncertainty of life, had disturbed the old fixed relations. The hope of every Egyptian turned to a glorified future life as Osiris.

The tendency to use magical texts and symbolic objects reached its height. About 700 B.C. a revival of national life, brought about by the establishment of the Egyptian kings of Sais as kings of Egypt, led to a renaissance of Egyptian art. The old monuments were copied and imitated, the old funerary texts and offering formulas were sought out in the older graves. Even the pyramid texts reappear after one thousand years of practical oblivion. The value of master words was so firmly fixed in the Egyptian mind that misunderstood texts of all sorts were copied out and placed in the graves to secure to the dead some vague benefit in the other world.

The process of mummification was at its height. The bodies were no longer preserved. The process was merely the creation of a simulacrum of the dead Osiris So-and-So. All the perishable parts of the body were removed or destroyed by chemicals. Only the skin, bones, hair, and teeth remained to be padded with mud and resin, wrapped in cloths, covered with a painted and gilded *cartonnage* to represent the glorified Osiris mummy.

VIII. THE PTOLEMAIC-ROMAN PERIOD

In the Ptolemaic-Roman period we see the final stage of the Osiris cult. Every dead man is laid in his grave without furniture, prepared as a simulacrum of Osiris. The wealthiest people have gilded and painted mummy cases with amulets and funerary papyrus. The poorer are merely bundles of wrappings. Every dead man is Osiris, and no doubt carried with him words learned on earth to gain his way to a place in the kingdom of Osiris. The offering places above the grave are still made and offerings are still brought.

To gain some idea of the way in which these two conceptions of the living dead were worked out in actual life, one has only to turn to the funerary customs of the modern Egyptians. In the case of both Christians and Moslems, the grave rites are similar; but with those of the Moslems I am more familiar. The grave consists still of the two parts, the burying place and the offering place. The swathed body is laid on the right side, with the right hand under the cheek and the face towards Mecca. At the burial the confession of the faith is recited over and over, lest the dead forget it. Korans are sometimes placed in the graves; and I have even seen a confession of the faith written on paper and placed on a twig before the face of the dead. At the appointed seasons-- especially at the great Feast of Sacrifice--offerings are brought to the grave. The family party passes through the cemetery, the women bearing baskets of bread and bottles of water, the men turning the head to the right and to the left and reciting the *fatha* in propitiation of the spirits. The party enters the offering inclosure of the grave of their relative. The wives greet the dead--"Peace unto thee, oh, my husband, oh, my father, we have wept until we have watered the earth with our tears on thy account." The offerings are laid before the tomb. A scribe is called and recites or reads some chapter of the Koran over and over, one hundred, one hundred and fifty, five hundred, one thousand times, and concludes: "I have read this for thee, oh, such and such a one." Or, "I have transferred the merit of this to thee." When you question these people as to the particulars of their belief, you find their ideas vague and indefinite. Among the men a dispute quickly starts,--the people who have been found good by the examining angels on the night of the burial are there, but the bad are somewhere else. No, says another, they are all in their graves, but the bad suffer torment. Still another maintains that the good have already passed to the lowest heaven. These are all mere remnants of theological discussions caught from the sheikhs. The women stolidly maintain that the dead are in their tombs and the offerings must be brought. When you inquire which are the good and which are the bad, there is again a great divergence of opinion; but it is clear that every man believes in his heart that a knowledge of the prayers and forms of the Moslem religion is absolutely essential and entirely sufficient to gain a desirable future life. The great master word is the confession of faith--there is no god but Allah and Mohammed is his prophet.

So it must have been in the last stage of the Osiris cult. Immortality, a glorified future existence as an Osiris in the kingdom of Osiris, with all the pleasures and comforts of life, was secured to him who was buried with the proper rites and knew the magic words. And yet the old feeling was never lost that the dead was somehow in the grave and might suffer hunger and thirst.

When Christianity came into Egypt, all the gaudy apparatus of the Osiris religion was swept out of existence. The body was to rise again and might not be mutilated. Mummification, which destroyed the body in order to preserve a conventional simulacrum, ceased abruptly. Grave furniture was of course unthinkable. But the use of charms did not cease. Crosses were embroidered in the gravecloths; or small crosses of metal or wood placed on the breast or arm; the gravestone bore a simple prayer to the Holy Spirit for the peaceful rest of the soul. But the offering place was still maintained; prayers were recited on the feast days; lamps were allowed to remain at the grave; food was brought, but given to the poor.

In all periods there are thousands of graves of poor people without a single thing to secure their future life,--people who were probably content simply to lay down the burdens of life. In the Christian period these thousands of unnamed dead all have one mark. They are laid with their feet to the east. Each one was a Christian and secure in his future life, according to his faith and his life on earth.

IX. SUMMARY

To sum up, the essential idea of the Egyptian conception of immortality was that the ghost or spirit of the man preserved the personality and the form of the man in the existence after death; that this spirit had the same desires, the same pleasures, the same necessities, and the same fears as on earth. Life after death was a duplicate of life on earth. On earth life depended on work, on getting food from the fields and the herds, on forming stone and metal, hide and vegetable fibre, into useful objects. In other words, life depended on human power over the natural materials of the earth. At the same time there were many things which could not be controlled by power over the earth and its elements,--the sting of the scorpion, the bite of the adder, the rise of the Nile, sickness, the sudden onslaught of the enemy, the straying of cattle, the disfavor of the god. For these evils man's only hope was magic,--the set words spoken in the proper manner which have power over all unseen influence. So in the case of life after death, all which human strength can provide of stores of grain and drink and garments must be secured for his use; but he must also be provided with the magic words to meet the chance evils of the future life.

It is not surprising that the unknown future presented to the imagination many evils unknown on earth. The spirit might forget its name, it might lose its heart, it might be bound fast by evil powers in the grave and unable to come forth by day. The mummy might decay; the spirit might forget its form. So, as time went on, the use of magic words became of greater and greater importance, until, to modern eyes, it seemed to overshadow all else in the Egyptian conception of life after death.

As a part of the magical provisions of the dead, the Osiris myth, probably built up in explanation of old rites, was drawn into the belief in a future life, and apparently at the beginning *solely for the benefit of the king*, for the benefit of those who claimed a certain divinity on earth. The earth-god Osiris, god of the living, had died and had been brought to life as god of the dead. So, also, the earth-king, the Horus, the son of Ra, must die, but he also would live again in the other world and share the throne of Osiris. More than this even, he became Osiris. He was admitted to the life of the gods. Of course the ideas of the existence of the gods were never clear and consistent. They lived in secret places, their whole life was mysterious as well as powerful. These are the field of knowledge which the Egyptian mind could not oversee with any satisfaction to itself. The most it could do was to formulate the magic words, invoking the names of the gods and conjuring them by the events in the Osiris myth to accept this king as Osiris. The exceptional man, the super-man, must have an exceptional future life; but to obtain it, he must have the knowledge of the names and words necessary to force the powers of the other world.

Thus the idea of an exceptional future life, a heaven, was brought into the Egyptian conception of life after death. Admission to it depended on the exceptional position on earth of those admitted. As even this exceptional position was only of avail when combined with the knowledge of certain formulas, it is not difficult to see how the knowledge of these formulas might be considered sufficient to obtain the better future life, even for others than the king. When in the depression that followed the extravagance of the pyramid age the central monarchy lost its power, Egypt broke up into a series of tribal baronies (nomes). In each was a ruler almost independent of the king, a man who might presume with the proper knowledge to claim a glorified future life similar to that of the king. And, indeed, we find from the burial inscriptions of the Middle Empire that such was the result. Feudalism extended the possibilities of heaven to the great nobles. In the New Empire, the royal power was gradually absorbed by the priestly organization of the national religion-- the religion of Amon-Ra; and the principle comes into practice that any priest having the necessary knowledge could obtain for himself an exceptional place in the future life. The Osirian burial customs spread even among the people. The swathed body extended on the back becomes universal, even though true mummification was still only for the rich.

In the Ptolemaic period, the preparation of all the apparatus of the Osiris burial was divided up into trades. Factories, one may say, turned out mummy cases of various kinds, with a scale of prices to fit every purse. Other factories turned out amulets and charms. Magical texts, the preparation of the body, the construction of the grave--all things were done by regular crafts. The cheapening of the apparatus is most striking. At the same time all but the poorest burials bear direct evidence of their character as Osiris burials.

On the side of the moral requirement we must not look too closely. There were powerful words which could compel even the great judges of the dead to return a favorable verdict. There were magic hearts of stone which might be worn in place of the heart, and, laid in the scales by Anubis, weigh heavier than the truth. One might by words compel Anubis to accept this stone heart instead of the real heart.

In general, one may say that the hope of immortality had little influence on the moral life of the ordinary Egyptian. The moral code was simple and sound and not greatly different from other primitive codes,--forbidding all those things which the body of men regard as unpleasant in others, commanding the plain virtues which were found pleasant in others. Here, again, I think we may well look to modern Egypt for a picture of ancient Egypt. We must not exaggerate the influence of the belief in immortality on general morality. We must not think too well of the life of the people--nor, on the other hand, too evil. They had their sins and their virtues. The common herd was driven by necessity and lived as it could. They clung to the belief in a life in the grave. The greater people had leisure to learn and to provide the magic necessary to secure a comfortable future life. They loved life and hated death.

Thus it was when the priests of the Osiris-Isis religion made their bid to the classical world. They offered immortality by initiation. Learn the proper rites, learn the master words, and secure eternal life among the great gods. It was a religion for the exceptional man down to the last; it required training and knowledge. Even in its most popular form in the Ptolemaic period, a specially instructed class was required, who sold for money the benefits of their knowledge, and men took rank in their security of future life according to their means.

Not until Christianity came, offering eternal life free and without price, did the common people find at last a road open to equal immortality with the great men of the earth.

The Codes Of Hammurabi And Moses
W. W. Davies

QTY

The discovery of the Hammurabi Code is one of the greatest achievements of archaeology, and is of paramount interest, not only to the student of the Bible, but also to all those interested in ancient history...

Religion   ISBN: *1-59462-338-4*   Pages:132
MSRP $12.95

The Theory of Moral Sentiments
Adam Smith

QTY

This work from 1749. contains original theories of conscience amd moral judgment and it is the foundation for systemof morals.

Philosophy   ISBN: *1-59462-777-0*   Pages:536
MSRP $19.95

Jessica's First Prayer
Hesba Stretton

QTY

In a screened and secluded corner of one of the many railway-bridges which span the streets of London there could be seen a few years ago, from five o'clock every morning until half past eight, a tidily set-out coffee-stall, consisting of a trestle and board, upon which stood two large tin cans, with a small fire of charcoal burning under each so as to keep the coffee boiling during the early hours of the morning when the work-people were thronging into the city on their way to their daily toil...

Childrens   ISBN: *1-59462-373-2*   Pages:84
MSRP $9.95

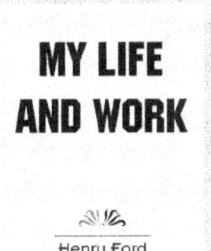

My Life and Work
Henry Ford

QTY

Henry Ford revolutionized the world with his implementation of mass production for the Model T automobile. Gain valuable business insight into his life and work with his own auto-biography... "We have only started on our development of our country we have not as yet, with all our talk of wonderful progress, done more than scratch the surface. The progress has been wonderful enough but..."

Biographies/   ISBN: *1-59462-198-5*   Pages:300
MSRP $21.95

www.bookjungle.com *email: sales@bookjungle.com fax: 630-214-0564 mail: Book Jungle PO Box 2226 Champaign, IL 61825*

The Art of Cross-Examination
Francis Wellman

QTY

I presume it is the experience of every author, after his first book is published upon an important subject, to be almost overwhelmed with a wealth of ideas and illustrations which could readily have been included in his book, and which to his own mind, at least, seem to make a second edition inevitable. Such certainly was the case with me; and when the first edition had reached its sixth impression in five months, I rejoiced to learn that it seemed to my publishers that the book had met with a sufficiently favorable reception to justify a second and considerably enlarged edition. ...

Reference   ISBN: *1-59462-647-2*

Pages:412

MSRP $19.95

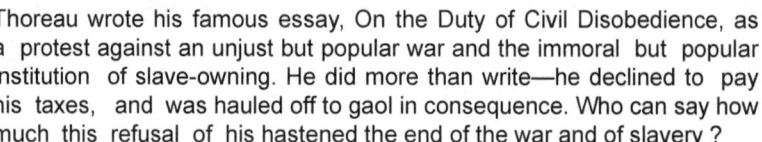

On the Duty of Civil Disobedience
Henry David Thoreau

QTY

Thoreau wrote his famous essay, On the Duty of Civil Disobedience, as a protest against an unjust but popular war and the immoral but popular institution of slave-owning. He did more than write—he declined to pay his taxes, and was hauled off to gaol in consequence. Who can say how much this refusal of his hastened the end of the war and of slavery ?

Law   ISBN: *1-59462-747-9*

Pages:48

MSRP $7.45

Dream Psychology Psychoanalysis for Beginners
Sigmund Freud

QTY

Sigmund Freud, born Sigismund Schlomo Freud (May 6, 1856 - September 23, 1939), was a Jewish-Austrian neurologist and psychiatrist who co-founded the psychoanalytic school of psychology. Freud is best known for his theories of the unconscious mind, especially involving the mechanism of repression; his redefinition of sexual desire as mobile and directed towards a wide variety of objects; and his therapeutic techniques, especially his understanding of transference in the therapeutic relationship and the presumed value of dreams as sources of insight into unconscious desires.

Psychology   ISBN: *1-59462-905-6*

Pages:196

MSRP $15.45

The Miracle of Right Thought
Orison Swett Marden

QTY

Believe with all of your heart that you will do what you were made to do. When the mind has once formed the habit of holding cheerful, happy, prosperous pictures, it will not be easy to form the opposite habit. It does not matter how improbable or how far away this realization may see, or how dark the prospects may be, if we visualize them as best we can, as vividly as possible, hold tenaciously to them and vigorously struggle to attain them, they will gradually become actualized, realized in the life. But a desire, a longing without endeavor, a yearning abandoned or held indifferently will vanish without realization.

Pages:360

Self Help   ISBN: *1-59462-644-8*

MSRP $25.45

QTY

The Rosicrucian Cosmo-Conception Mystic Christianity *by Max Heindel*   ISBN: *1-59462-188-8*   **$38.95**
The Rosicrucian Cosmo-conception is not dogmatic, neither does it appeal to any other authority than the reason of the student. It is: not controversial, but is: sent forth in the, hope that it may help to clear...   New Age/Religion Pages 646

Abandonment To Divine Providence *by Jean-Pierre de Caussade*   ISBN: *1-59462-228-0*   **$25.95**
"The Rev. Jean Pierre de Caussade was one of the most remarkable spiritual writers of the Society of Jesus in France in the 18th Century. His death took place at Toulouse in 1751. His works have gone through many editions and have been republished...   Inspirational/Religion Pages 400

Mental Chemistry *by Charles Haanel*   ISBN: *1-59462-192-6*   **$23.95**
Mental Chemistry allows the change of material conditions by combining and appropriately utilizing the power of the mind. Much like applied chemistry creates something new and unique out of careful combinations of chemicals the mastery of mental chemistry...   New Age Pages 354

The Letters of Robert Browning and Elizabeth Barret Barrett 1845-1846 vol II   ISBN: *1-59462-193-4*   **$35.95**
by Robert Browning and Elizabeth Barrett   Biographies Pages 596

Gleanings In Genesis (volume I) *by Arthur W. Pink*   ISBN: *1-59462-130-6*   **$27.45**
Appropriately has Genesis been termed "the seed plot of the Bible" for in it we have, in germ form, almost all of the great doctrines which are afterwards fully developed in the books of Scripture which follow...   Religion/Inspirational Pages 420

The Master Key *by L. W. de Laurence*   ISBN: *1-59462-001-6*   **$30.95**
In no branch of human knowledge has there been a more lively increase of the spirit of research during the past few years than in the study of Psychology, Concentration and Mental Discipline. The requests for authentic lessons in Thought Control, Mental Discipline and...   New Age/Business Pages 422

The Lesser Key Of Solomon Goetia *by L. W. de Laurence*   ISBN: *1-59462-092-X*   **$9.95**
This translation of the first book of the "Lernegton" which is now for the first time made accessible to students of Talismanic Magic was done, after careful collation and edition, from numerous Ancient Manuscripts in Hebrew, Latin, and French...   New Age/Occult Pages 92

Rubaiyat Of Omar Khayyam *by Edward Fitzgerald*   ISBN:*1-59462-332-5*   **$13.95**
Edward Fitzgerald, whom the world has already learned, in spite of his own efforts to remain within the shadow of anonymity, to look upon as one of the rarest poets of the century, was born at Bredfield, in Suffolk, on the 31st of March, 1809. He was the third son of John Purcell...   Music Pages 172

Ancient Law *by Henry Maine*   ISBN: *1-59462-128-4*   **$29.95**
The chief object of the following pages is to indicate some of the earliest ideas of mankind, as they are reflected in Ancient Law, and to point out the relation of those ideas to modern thought.   Religion/History Pages 452

Far-Away Stories *by William J. Locke*   ISBN: *1-59462-129-2*   **$19.45**
"Good wine needs no bush, but a collection of mixed vintages does. And this book is just such a collection. Some of the stories I do not want to remain buried for ever in the museum files of dead magazine-numbers an author's not unpardonable vanity..."   Fiction Pages 272

Life of David Crockett *by David Crockett*   ISBN: *1-59462-250-7*   **$27.45**
"Colonel David Crockett was one of the most remarkable men of the times in which he lived. Born in humble life, but gifted with a strong will, an indomitable courage, and unremitting perseverance...   Biographies/New Age Pages 424

Lip-Reading *by Edward Nitchie*   ISBN: *1-59462-206-X*   **$25.95**
Edward B. Nitchie, founder of the New York School for the Hard of Hearing, now the Nitchie School of Lip-Reading, Inc, wrote "LIP-READING Principles and Practice". The development and perfecting of this meritorious work on lip-reading was an undertaking...   How-to Pages 400

A Handbook of Suggestive Therapeutics, Applied Hypnotism, Psychic Science   ISBN: *1-59462-214-0*   **$24.95**
by Henry Munro   Health/New Age/Health/Self-help Pages 376

A Doll's House: and Two Other Plays *by Henrik Ibsen*   ISBN: *1-59462-112-8*   **$19.95**
Henrik Ibsen created this classic when in revolutionary 1848 Rome. Introducing some striking concepts in playwriting for the realist genre, this play has been studied the world over.   Fiction/Classics/Plays 308

The Light of Asia *by sir Edwin Arnold*   ISBN: *1-59462-204-3*   **$13.95**
In this poetic masterpiece, Edwin Arnold describes the life and teachings of Buddha. The man who was to become known as Buddha to the world was born as Prince Gautama of India but he rejected the worldly riches and abandoned the reigns of power when... Religion/History/Biographies Pages 170

The Complete Works of Guy de Maupassant *by Guy de Maupassant*   ISBN: *1-59462-157-8*   **$16.95**
"For days and days, nights and nights, I had dreamed of that first kiss which was to consecrate our engagement, and I knew not on what spot I should put my lips..."   Fiction/Classics Pages 240

The Art of Cross-Examination *by Francis L. Wellman*   ISBN: *1-59462-309-0*   **$26.95**
Written by a renowned trial lawyer, Wellman imparts his experience and uses case studies to explain how to use psychology to extract desired information through questioning.   How-to/Science/Reference Pages 408

Answered or Unanswered? *by Louisa Vaughan*   ISBN: *1-59462-248-5*   **$10.95**
Miracles of Faith in China   Religion Pages 112

The Edinburgh Lectures on Mental Science (1909) *by Thomas*   ISBN: *1-59462-008-3*   **$11.95**
This book contains the substance of a course of lectures recently given by the writer in the Queen Street Hall, Edinburgh. Its purpose is to indicate the Natural Principles governing the relation between Mental Action and Material Conditions...   New Age/Psychology Pages 148

Ayesha *by H. Rider Haggard*   ISBN: *1-59462-301-5*   **$24.95**
Verily and indeed it is the unexpected that happens! Probably if there was one person upon the earth from whom the Editor of this, and of a certain previous history, did not expect to hear again...   Classics Pages 380

Ayala's Angel *by Anthony Trollope*   ISBN: *1-59462-352-X*   **$29.95**
The two girls were both pretty, but Lucy who was twenty-one who supposed to be simple and comparatively unattractive, whereas Ayala was credited, as her Bombwhat romantic name might show, with poetic charm and a taste for romance. Ayala when her father died was nineteen...   Fiction Pages 484

The American Commonwealth *by James Bryce*   ISBN: *1-59462-286-8*   **$34.45**
An interpretation of American democratic political theory. It examines political mechanics and society from the perspective of Scotsman James Bryce   Politics Pages 572

Stories of the Pilgrims *by Margaret P. Pumphrey*   ISBN: *1-59462-116-0*   **$17.95**
This book explores pilgrims religious oppression in England as well as their escape to Holland and eventual crossing to America on the Mayflower, and their early days in New England...   History Pages 268

QTY

The Fasting Cure *by Sinclair Upton* ISBN: *1-59462-222-1* **$13.95**
In the Cosmopolitan Magazine for May, 1910, and in the Contemporary Review (London) for April, 1910, I published an article dealing with my experi-ences in fasting. I have written a great many magazine articles, but never one which attracted so much attention... New Age/Self Help/Health Pages 164

Hebrew Astrology *by Sepharial* ISBN: *1-59462-308-2* **$13.45**
In these days of advanced thinking it is a matter of common observation that we have left many of the old landmarks behind and that we are now pressing forward to greater heights and to a wider horizon than that which represented the mind-content of our progenitors... Astrology Pages 144

Thought Vibration or The Law of Attraction in the Thought World ISBN: *1-59462-127-6* **$12.95**

by William Walker Atkinson *Psychology/Religion Pages 144*

Optimism *by Helen Keller* ISBN: *1-59462-108-X* **$15.95**
Helen Keller was blind, deaf, and mute since 19 months old, yet famously learned how to overcome these handicaps, communicate with the world, and spread her lectures promoting optimism. An inspiring read for everyone... Biographies/Inspirational Pages 84

Sara Crewe *by Frances Burnett* ISBN: *1-59462-360-0* **$9.45**
In the first place, Miss Minchin lived in London. Her home was a large, dull, tall one, in a large, dull square, where all the houses were alike, and all the sparrows were alike, and where all the door-knockers made the same heavy sound... Childrens/Classic Pages 88

The Autobiography of Benjamin Franklin *by Benjamin Franklin* ISBN: *1-59462-135-7* **$24.95**
The Autobiography of Benjamin Franklin has probably been more extensively read than any other American historical work, and no other book of its kind has had such ups and downs of fortune. Franklin lived for many years in England, where he was agent... Biographies/History Pages 332

Name	
Email	
Telephone	
Address	
City, State ZIP	

☐ **Credit Card**   ☐ **Check / Money Order**

Credit Card Number	
Expiration Date	
Signature	

Please Mail to: Book Jungle
PO Box 2226
Champaign, IL 61825
or Fax to: 630-214-0564

ORDERING INFORMATION

web: *www.bookjungle.com*
email: *sales@bookjungle.com*
fax: *630-214-0564*
mail: *Book Jungle PO Box 2226 Champaign, IL 61825*
or PayPal *to sales@bookjungle.com*

Please contact us for bulk discounts

DIRECT-ORDER TERMS

**20% Discount if You Order
Two or More Books**
Free Domestic Shipping!
Accepted: Master Card, Visa,
Discover, American Express

www.ingramcontent.com/pod-product-compliance
Lightning Source LLC
Chambersburg PA
CBHW081202170626
46813CB00009B/3292